A Hero's Journey

A Mayan Myth of Self-Discovery

Pamela J Peck, PhD

Order this book online at www.trafford.com
or email orders@trafford.com

Most Trafford titles are also available at major online book retailers.

Illustrated by Pamela J Peck
Cover design by Pamela J Peck
Edited by Ken Johnson

Print information available on the last page.

ISBN: 978-1-4907-7447-3 (sc)
ISBN: 978-1-4907-7446-6 (e)

Trafford rev.   05/31/2017

 www.trafford.com

North America & international
toll-free: 1 888 232 4444 (USA & Canada)
fax: 812 355 4082

A Hero's Journey

Pamela J Peck

To the hero in all of us

ABOUT THE JOURNEY

This modern mythology was originally written by the author as part of a Lecture Series for a trans-Atlantic crossing from Fort Lauderdale to Barcelona on Royal Caribbean's flagship *Legend of the Seas* in May of 1999.

Only the story portions of the lectures are included here, their purpose being not only to share history and culture of the geographical areas but to point to a much wider purpose: illumination of anthropologist Joseph Campbell's teachings about the mythological Hero's Journey.

THE JOURNEY

ABOUT THE JOURNAL

Latitude	26° N
Longitude	80° W

For this publication, the anthropologist is sharing her personal experience of the voyage by interweaving Journal entries alongside the mythological story. The author also shares material on the ports of call she has both researched in advance and discovered along the way.

The seven entries of the Hero story — an integral part of the overall Lecture Series on the mythological Hero's Journey — were delivered aboard ship on days at sea.

THE JOURNAL

In the Year
One Thousand, Nine Hundred
And Ninety-Nine

THE JOURNEY

Prologue
A HERO'S JOURNEY

Imagine if you will, a sea of islands with Spanish names and Spanish traditions, yet laying an ocean away from Spain. And imagine, at the westerly edge of that sea of islands, a narrow strip of land, stretching more than 2000 miles, connecting two great continents. In the north it is a broad hilly plateau, and it swings southeastward to jumbled peaks edged by coastal lowlands. Here nature created a landscape of infinite variety — from dense rain forest to stark desert plain, from steamy marshes to snowy peaks. And here an ancient people molded spectacular cultures that rose and fell between 2000 BCE and the 16th century of the current era. That is when the Spaniards arrived and overpowered the civilizations they found.

Imagine now a boy, about to become a man, who grows up in this favored place, a descendant of a great people known as the Maya. It is 500 years later, the final year before a new millennium. The boy has heard the stories of greatness about his cultural past, how as early as 5000 BCE, farmers domesticated corn and beans, and laid the foundation for a settled life; how trade networks were set up to link the farming villages; how his ancestors came to know and use astronomy, writing and the calendar; and how religion inspired art and architecture and gave them a pantheon of gods. His people had built great cities and temples and had fashioned beautiful ornaments and jewelry from gold.

But that was gone now: cities and temples reduced to rubble; the tribe, powerless and poor. They had lost their greatness, the boy had often heard his elders lament, because they had lost their gold. So the boy determined that when he grew to be a man, he would leave the home tribe and go in search of it.

The boy knew little of the outside world. But he did learn something of the people who came for the gold. That story he was taught in school.

It started with an Italian navigator, they said, who sailed in the service of Spain. Cristobal Colon, they called him in Spanish. He set out with a fleet of three small ships to find a westward sea route to Asia. The Spanish were in search of such a route, he was told, because they wanted to trade in silk and spices with China. But Cristobal never reached China. Instead he landed on the shores of a new world and returned to Spain a year later, not with silk and spices, but with gold.

Cristobal made four voyages to this New World, the boy learned, establishing Spanish colonies in the Caribbean and exploring the coastline of what anthropologists would come to know as Mesoamerica. But that was just the beginning. His discoveries led to fleets of Spanish ships exploring and inhabiting the Caribbean, and Central and South America. One Spaniard, named Hernan Cortes, would lead the conquest of Mexico, and another, Francisco Pizarro, would conquer Peru. Many Spaniards came to the New World and returned with the gold of Columbia and Ecuador, of Hispaniola and Panama.

Imagine now it is the month of May, past the spring equinox but not yet the summer solstice. The boy has bid farewell to the home tribe and has set out to recover its lost fortune. He earns passage as a cabin boy on a ship that is crossing the Atlantic, bound for Spain. In two weeks time, the ship will dock in Barcelona. The boy believes this is the place where he will find and recover the lost gold. For Barcelona is the city where Cristobal was received by Queen Isabella and King Ferdinand when he first returned to Spain with the precious yellow metal.

And so a hero's journey begins ....

THE JOURNAL

Latitude   26° N
Longitude   80° W

DAY 0.   FORT LAUDERDALE

1:00 p.m.: I arrived in Fort Lauderdale last night and boarded the ship early this morning. I have a very comfortable and well-appointed stateroom on the starboard of the ship, which right now offers a fine view of the dockside. While I was getting settled in my stateroom, the cabin attendant came by to introduce himself and to find out if I had need of anything. He is a young boy from the interior of Mexico, and this is his first contract. I shall make him the "hero" figure for my mythological Lecture Series.

From my stateroom window I see passengers

making their way up the gangway with their carry-on luggage. Their large bags have been collected on the dockside, to be boarded later. Alongside the stacks of suitcases, crate upon crate of foodstuffs are sitting on the dock, and still more crates are being offloaded from a number of huge transport trucks. Can passengers and crew possibly consume this much food on a two-week trans-Atlantic voyage!

4:00 p.m.: Most of the crates and luggage have been boarded now, and I have unpacked my clothing and hung my gowns. I think I have perhaps brought too many pairs of shoes — but can a girl ever have too many pairs of shoes ....

10:00 p.m.: The "Legend of the Seas" pulled away from her moorings shortly after 6:00 p.m. I watched from the deck as she made her way through the channel and moved into the open sea. From their homes along the waterway, people waved as we cruised by. I felt an air of adventure about leaving a continent, knowing that I would be crossing an ocean. How easily such a voyage can be accomplished today compared to that of early explorations!

THE JOURNAL

Latitude   23° N
Longitude   79° W

DAY 1.   AT SEA

4:00 p.m.: Our first day at sea. The ocean is quite calm and passengers are settling into the rhythm of being aboard a cruise ship. The ship itself is very beautiful with an open centrum mid-ship and stunning artwork throughout. A 70,000-tonne vessel, she can accommodate more than 2,000 guests. Her maiden voyage was in 1995.

There are a myriad of activities from which to choose. As for me, I am polishing my lecture material in preparation for my first lecture tomorrow. I am feeling especially fortunate because my stateroom attendant is turning out to be the perfect "hero" for my story.

Right now we are cruising through the Caribbean Sea, a vast body of water containing a myriad of islands. Most cruises to this area begin in Fort Lauderdale or Miami. Some start in San Juan, Puerto Rico, and the ships cruise to different areas. The Western Caribbean includes destinations like Jamaica, Grand Cayman, and Cozumel. Eastern Mediterranean cruises usually include the Virgin Islands or the Bahamas, and Southern Caribbean cruises usually make their way to the Lesser Antilles, the Venezuelan coast, Martinique, Barbados and Curacao. We are tracking a southeasterly course that will take us between Cuba and the Bahamas toward our first port of call at St. Thomas in the US Virgin Islands.

I have a guidebook with me appropriately called "Caribbean by Cruise Ship". I learn that Amerindian tribes, including the Arawak and the Carib, first inhabited the islands. They came from around the Amazon basin from where they migrated to the north coast of South America before arriving in the Caribbean.

By the time Columbus appeared in 1492, the Carib and Arawak had settled most of the Caribbean. But with a difference. The Arawak were peaceful, and seemed content with simple housing and a plentiful food supply. They lived in brush houses and grew root crops by planting cuttings in mounds of earth. They slept on woven nets strung between the trees, which they called hammocks, the same word by which these nets are known today. They made pottery and wove baskets, and made cotton clothing; they had stone tools and jewelry — rings, necklaces and masks — shaped from small amounts of gold found in the local riverbeds. They also played games like soccer, and built playing courts like those of the influential Maya.

The Arawak were organized as a loose federation of provinces within an island group, each village with a local headman. More than that, there was equality between the genders; women were equal to men in most areas.

The same cannot be said for the Carib. Tasks between the genders were strictly defined and men treated their wives as servants. They were aggressive; they pushed the Arawak away from the more appealing islands. And while the Arawak welcomed the first Spaniards with open arms, the Carib resisted any attempt to conquer or enslave them. They were fearless and powerful — enough to defeat Europeans in battle. They also developed a reputation for cannibalism, even though human flesh was not a part of their regular diet.

Of course, these native tribes are no more. The impact of Spanish settlement devastated the

Arawak. By the end of the 16ᵗʰ century, they were extinct. As for the Carib, those in Grenada sold some of their land to the French in exchange for knives and baubles. They soon realized they had entered into a bad deal and tried to rectify it, but their attempt at rebellion was swiftly put down. With defeat all but certain, those Carib remaining — men, women and children — threw themselves over a cliff.

The Spanish ... the Dutch ... the English ... the French .... The struggle for control ... the scourge of slavery ... the struggle for freedom — such is the turbulent history of the Caribbean. Today each island shows its unique character and culture. That, coupled with tropical climate and plenty of sunshine, makes the Caribbean a magnet for the scores of cruise ships that ply these waters.

THE JOURNAL

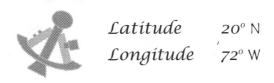

Latitude 20° N
Longitude 72° W

DAY 2. AT SEA

Our second day at sea. We continue on our southeasterly course and are now closer to the Dominican Republic and Puerto Rico. The seas are quite calm with a few swells.

Tomorrow we shall arrive at the island of St. Thomas in the US Virgin Islands. My guidebook tells me that Christopher Columbus named these islands in 1493 from the legend of Saint Ursula and her 11,000 virgin martyrs. In 1917, the

United States bought the islands from Denmark for $25 million — not for the sunshine or beaches but to protect American shipping interests.

The capital of the Virgin Islands is the town of Charlotte Amalie on the south coast of St. Thomas. The town began in 1672 when the Danish West India Company began a settlement there. Fort Christian, it was called then, and it soon belied its name by quickly becoming a slave-trading centre. The springing up of an abundance of taverns soon earned it the name "Taphus" (Beer Hall) until it was officially declared a town in 1691 and given the name of Charlotte Amalie, in honour of the Danish Queen.

This information was very useful to me this morning, allowing me to weave local history and culture into my story based on Joseph Campbell's mythological hero's journey. As the

Lecture Series progresses, it will be rewarding and fun to watch as the passengers eventually discover that the hero figure, while modeled on my stateroom attendant, is really each one of them. They need only use their imaginations.

THE JOURNEY

Part I
GOING FOR GOLD
A Voyage of Discovery

Imagine if you will, that it is night and the *Legend of the Seas* has left her port on the southeasterly tip of North America. The ship plies the open water of the sea of islands bearing Spanish names. There is silence apart from the gentle splashing of waves against the ship's bow. Most of the passengers are asleep — but not the boy. He wanders along the outside deck, staring into the sky.

The boy knew a few things about gold. But why, he wonders, could it cause the rise and fall of the home tribe. After all, there were many different metals; what was so special about this one. He had asked that question of a headmaster in the town where he learned to speak a limited but respectable English. The master had explained that gold is malleable and naturally occurs in a pure state, which means it can be worked by simple hammering. Because of this, he explained, gold was used in the earliest known civilizations like Mesopotamia, Egypt, Persia and Crete and that it was hammered into ornaments and jewelry in Egypt as far back as 3000 BCE. So gold became the measure of wealth and of power.

This answer didn't entirely satisfy because his own ancestors had also made gold ornaments and jewelry thousands of years ago. Why didn't they use other metals like silver? Because, the master had explained, silver comes compounded with other substances. It couldn't be used until smelting was discovered in the Bronze Age. And by that time, gold had come to be used as money.

The boy knew about money too. His tribe had money. Paper money. And it was worth next to nothing. So when the Spaniards took the gold from the tribes, he now wanted to know, were the tribes left only with the paper money?

No, the master had explained. First, gold was used as money, but gold is cumbersome to carry around so somebody got the idea to print gold values on paper notes and keep the real gold stored in a safe place. The person with those paper notes could then exchange them for items worth their printed value. Gold was thereafter a standard for money rather than money itself.

So now the boy wanted to know if the gold belonging to the home tribe was being kept for them in a safe place somewhere. And again the master had said no, explaining that after awhile there were so many paper notes printed that there was not enough gold to cover their value. So gold became a symbol.

The boy didn't understand how gold could be a symbol. And he didn't much care because he wasn't interested in symbols. He didn't want symbolic gold and he didn't want paper gold. He wanted real gold. For only real gold would restore the lost power of the home tribe.

Imagine now that the ship's navigator finishes his watch on the bridge. He heads toward his quarters, then notices the boy standing alone on the deck, and approaches.

"You are new on the ship."

"Yes, sir."

"And how long is your contract?"

"No contract, sir. I will leave the ship in Barcelona."

"Barcelona. And what is your business there?"

"I am going to bring home the gold."

"Ah, you are an athlete."

The boy doesn't know that word. He notices the navigator wears a pendant that looks like gold. It is hammered in the shape of a crown and anchor.

"That is gold?" the boy wants to know.

"Well, it's a symbol of gold."

Ah, thinks the boy. On this ship they use the new kind of gold — the symbolic kind.

"I will bring back real gold," the boy states.

"They will be very proud of you."

"But first I must find it."

"Well, if it is gold you seek," suggests the navigator, "you need not sail all the way to Barcelona. There is plenty of gold in the Virgin Islands, and the ship will arrive there after only two days' sailing."

Ah, thinks the boy, maybe that is the safe place where the Spaniards store the gold.

"Did a man named Cristobal Colon go to these Virgin Islands?" the boy asks.

"They say he discovered the place," comes the reply. "He sailed there on his second voyage to the New World. But there were people already living there when he arrived so I don't think we can say he really discovered the place. There were people there as early as 2500 BCE."

"And more Spaniards came?" asks the boy.

"Spaniards, then other Europeans from France, England, Holland and Denmark. The Virgin Islands attracted more foreign powers than any of these islands. Tropical climate, beautiful scenery .... And they wanted them for other purposes too. Like St. Thomas where the ship will be docking. It was once a slave-trading post, then a refuge for pirates. And the islands became even more valuable once they built the Panama Canal."

The boy is silent. He just wants to know about gold. But this man talks about other things. "All that has changed now," the navigator goes on. "The buccaneers have been replaced by merchants. But you can still see old buildings and sights that will take you back in time. Like the Danish architecture — old warehouses where the treasure of marauding pirates was stashed away centuries ago. Now they are fashionable shops and trendy restaurants. That's why most people go there today."

"But where's the gold?" the boy wants to know.

"When we arrive, go to the Main Street of the town which runs parallel to the harbour. It is lined with gold."

"I heard about a place where the streets are paved with gold. Is this the place?" asks the boy.

"That's a different place. And Main Street is not paved with gold. It's lined with gold. The gold is in the shop windows on either side of the street. Gold — and diamonds too."

"No, I don't want diamonds. Diamonds you would need to sell in order to get gold. With the gold you can turn it into anything you want."

"And what do you want to turn it into?"

"Cooking pots and farming tools."

"Interesting, you want to turn gold into base metal while some people spend a lifetime trying to turn base metal into gold. Why not just buy the pots and tools with money?"

"Our money is worthless. That's why I need to get gold."

"Well," says the navigator, "To get gold in St. Thomas, you're going to need plastic."

"You can get gold with plastic?" the boy questions.

"Sure. That's what a lot of the people on this ship will be doing."

The boy is confused. The navigator looks him in the eye. "You say you have no gold, and that is true for you because you think it is so."

"But if I have gold already, where is it?"

"That is what you must discover for yourself."

"In St. Thomas?" the boy asks.

The navigator thinks for a moment. "Imagine," he says, "you are given the choice between two things. The first is metallic gold, hammered into bricks and stacked to form a wall. The second is a record of all the great ideas in the history of the world, from the earliest to the most recent, preserved on paper notes and stacked to form a pyramid. Which would you choose?"

"I would choose the brick wall," the boy replies without hesitation, "Because I am only interested in real gold."

The navigator is silent, and then he speaks. "If you are serious about seeking real gold, there is something I want you to do when we get to St. Thomas. Look for a passageway, a narrow corridor that runs between the Main Street and the harbour. It is not for everyone to know. To enter, you must tell them that you have passage on *Legend of the Seas*. You may take rest there from the heat of the day, and if you are lucky, you will find there something that will lead you to real gold."

"In a narrow corridor?"

"About half way along Main Street."

"Between Main Street and the harbour?"

"Yes, Charlotte Amalie."

"I ask for Charlotte Amalie?"

"No, no. That's the name of the town where the ship will dock. It used to be called 'Taphus' which means 'Beer Hall' because the taverns were very popular with the rough and tumble seamen who called at St. Thomas. The island was Danish then, and they renamed the town 'Charlotte Amalie' in honour of the king's wife."

The boy grows pensive. "The merchants of Charlotte Amalie, with all that gold. They must be very rich."

"Well, they keep a lot of the precious metal under cover," offers the navigator, "but whether or not they are rich I cannot say." And with that he bids the cabin boy goodnight.

THE JOURNAL

 Latitude   18° N

Longitude   65° W

DAY 3.   ST. THOMAS, USVI

We tied up to the dock at the cruise terminal in St. Thomas early this morning. Actually, there are two terminals in St. Thomas. We are at the main one, located on the east side of the harbour, not far from downtown.

St. Thomas is not very big — only 13 miles long and four miles wide so it's not difficult to get to the beaches. But I didn't head to the beaches; I made my way into the town of Charlotte Amalie.

The main streets run parallel to the harbour, with many interlocking side streets and alleys, all framed by old colonial buildings. It must look today very much as it did in the 1800's when Charlotte Amalie was one of the principal trading centres in the West Indies. At that time it would have been filled with the crews of merchant ships, whalers, fishermen and naval personnel. Today it is bustling with cruise passengers, crowding into a plethora of up-scale duty-free shops and colorful boutiques.

There are some interesting sites well worth a visit, like the Legislative Building, the seat of the U.S. Virgin Islands Senate. It is a green two-storey building of Italian Renaissance design. Then there is Fort Christian, the oldest standing structure on the island. Emancipation Garden commemorates the freeing of the slaves in 1848 and is the site of many official ceremonies. Government House is a three-storey building in the neo-classical design. Ninety-nine steps lead up the hillside behind Government House. Standing on top of Government Hill is Skysborg, a five-storey cone-shaped stone tower constructed by the Danish in 1678. Now part of a hotel, the tower is also referred to as Blackbeard's Castle because it is said that infamous pirate stayed there.

It was very warm in Charlotte Amalie, even in the early morning hours. Being as it is only the month of May, I can well imagine how high the temperatures must reach in the mid-summer. Historically, wealthy merchants lived in the surrounding hillsides where they could enjoy the cool sea breezes and magnificent views of the harbour while their import warehouses lined the waterfront below.

After a day of exploring the town, including a climb of the 99 steps to Government Hill, I returned to the air-conditioned comfort of the ship. Some of the ladies were sporting new pieces of jewelry. One of them showed me her very large new amethyst ring and confided that she had paid $1,000 less for it than she expected to pay. I didn't tell her that my sole purchase was an inexpensive silver chain!

THE JOURNAL

Latitude   22° N
Longitude   53° W

DAY 4.   AT SEA

We are at sea once again, this time setting an easterly course into the Atlantic Ocean. The Caribbean Sea will soon be behind us now, along with those island groups that fan out in a convex pattern from the U.S. Virgin Islands to the continent of South America — Guadeloupe, Martinique, Dominica, St. Lucia, Grenada ... all the way down to Trinidad and Tobago before touching the shores of Venezuela. Looking out into that vast expanse of water, I feel propelled into another world. And although I know the area has long been mapped and charted, and that many have passed this way before me, I feel as though I am sailing into the unknown.

I presented the second in my Lecture Series today. It reminded me to look into the night sky. So tonight, I wandered along the outside deck, staring at the brilliant stars. They glisten as stars can only when distanced from the lights of human habitation. It was a marvel — and a mystery — to behold.

THE JOURNEY

Part II

STAR VOYAGERS

Where Science and Mythology Converge

Imagine if you will, the *Legend of the Seas* pulling away from her berth in St. Thomas and heading into the open sea. Imagine the passengers soaking their feet in the solarium after a glorious day of shopping for gold in Charlotte Amalie. Night falls; the navigator plots his position and sets an easterly course from the bridge. The winds are calm; the sea is mild.

Imagine now the navigator ends his watch and walks along the outside deck. He knew the cabin boy would return to the ship in St. Thomas, so he is not surprised to see him once again standing there alone, staring at the sky. He walks up to the boy. "Did you find your gold in St. Thomas?" he asks.

"They told me the gold is on the ship," the boy replies.

"Ah, you found that special place I told you about. In the narrow passageway between the Main Street and the harbour. And you told them you were from the good ship, *Legend of the Seas*. Right?"

The boy nods.

"And . . .?"

"They said, 'Follow your legend'. This is the *Legend*. So I came back to the ship."

"Did they say anything else?"

"No, they just said 'Follow your legend and it will lead to gold.' "

The navigator pauses. "I wonder how many others on the ship are here to follow their legend," he muses to himself, then turns his attention back to the boy. "Do you know what a legend is?" he asks.

The boy says he doesn't.

The navigator points to the sky. "Look up there, " he says. "Tell me what you see."

"Stars," the boy replies.

"Anything else?"

"A black sky."

"I see a map," states the navigator.

"A map, sir?"

"Yes, you see, when people got the idea to venture across the oceans, they used the stars to navigate between their own countries and distant ports. They made maps of the stars and used the maps to guide their journeys."

The boy stares into the sky. "I don't see any maps."

"It all depends on the way you look at it. You have to see with your imagination. Like the ancient Egyptians. They divided the brighter stars into groups. Later the

Greeks did the same thing. And maybe they had a better imagination because these are the groups we still use today."

The navigator points overhead. "The most familiar one here in the northern sky is *Ursa Major* — the Great Bear of mythology. It's springtime now, so Ursa Major is almost directly overhead. Some people know it as the Big Dipper because those seven bright stars form the shape of a saucepan. Now, the two stars opposite the handle point to *Polaris*, the North Star. That star is always north. If you were at the North Pole, it would be directly overhead. So once navigators find *Polaris*, they know where north is and they can set their course by it."

The boy gazes at the stars as the navigator talks on.

"There are star maps in the southern hemisphere too. But because civilization began and developed first in the northern hemisphere, early astronomers did not know the southern stars. It was not until people voyaged southward in search of riches and new territories that these stars were charted. The most distinctive southern constellation is called the *Crux Australis* — the Southern Cross . . . four very bright stars form the shape of a cross.

"Now, when the Polynesians first traveled north in their large dugout canoes, like from French Polynesia to the Hawaiian Islands, the Southern Cross gradually disappeared from view and they saw the North Star for the very first time. They must have been fascinated by this bright star that did not move."

"So a legend is a map of the stars," the boy says, "for steering ships and canoes?"

"That's one way of looking at it," the navigator replies. "But there's another way. Look at *Polaris* again. Now let your eye follow down to those stars that look like a 'w'. That's *Cassiopeia*. Above *Cassiopeia*, that cluster is *Cepheus*. Next, look across from *Cassiopeia* to the next bright cluster; that's *Andromeda*. At a point below and between these two last clusters is one called *Perseus*. You would be able to see this constellation better in winter because then all the stars are above the horizon. Now, there is a great story about these stars.

"In Greek mythology, the great god, Zeus, in the guise of a shower of gold, comes to a woman and makes her the mother of Perseus. But the woman's father learns from the oracle of Delphi that his daughter will have a son who will grow up to kill his grandfather, which is himself. So the man locks his daughter and Perseus into a chest and throws the chest into the sea.

"Perseus and his mother — inside the chest — wash up on the shore of a kingdom. The king there falls in love with the woman but doesn't want her son around. So the king tricks the young Perseus into going on a dangerous mission to the extremities of the earth where there are dreaded monsters and sea serpents. After a very long time and many difficult encounters, Perseus finally achieves the impossible mission.

"On his way back home, Perseus reaches Ethiopia and finds the country in a state of desolation. Cassiopeia, wife of King Cepheus of Ethiopia, upsets the sea god Neptune by boasting that she is more beautiful than the sea-nymphs. Neptune gets angry and sends a very mean monster to terrorize the kingdom. In their terror, the

Ethiopians appeal to their god in the desert who explains that Neptune will be appeased only if Cepheus will sacrifice his daughter Andromeda to the monster. Sadly, the king agrees and Andromeda is chained to a rock.

"Perseus comes along and finds the unhappy Andromeda chained to the rock, awaiting death — and he falls in love with her at first sight. So, with great difficulty, he kills the monster, saves Andromeda and marries her. Perseus then takes Andromeda back to the place where he has left his mother with the jealous king, only to find that his mother is being persecuted. So with more great difficulty, he frees his mother by turning her persecutors into stone, then returns to his birthplace with his mother and his wife.

"Now the grandfather, remembering what the oracle had said long ago, flees when he sees Perseus. But, you see, it is written in the stars. And one day, Perseus is throwing the discus during some athletic games where his grandfather is present, and the discus strikes and kills the old man. Perseus is now in line to succeed to his grandfather's throne — which he doesn't want — so he has to go away again and establish his family in another place. Which he does — and this is the family into which the hero Hercules is later born.

"Now, this legend is not a map for a ship's journey," the navigator continues. "It's a map for a human journey. The hero, Perseus, is forced to leave his familiar world and venture into the unknown. It takes him into strange worlds where he encounters many difficulties. In the process of overcoming the difficulties he becomes a man. If he did not leave home and take the journey, he would not grow into responsible manhood. So the important thing is the journey, not the destination."

This is not what the boy wants to hear; the only thing on his mind is the destination.

"It's the hero's journey," the navigator explains, "and it appears again and again in mythology. There's Homer's *Odyssey*, written in Greek in the 6th century BCE. The hero, Odysseus, is detained on an island under the rule of the sea-nymph Calypso — which means 'concealer'. The god Zeus persuades Calypso to let him go. Odysseus makes his escape on a raft which Zeus tells him how to construct, then spends a long and perilous time at sea before he eventually arrives, unconscious, to the place of his birth.

"There's Virgil's *Aeneid*, written in Latin, in the 1st century CE. Here we meet the hero Aeneis in the burning ruins of Troy, prepared to fight to his death. But a dream tells him to flee the battle and to found a new Troy in a distant land across the sea. So carrying his household gods, Aeneis escapes from the ruins, and there follows seven long years of treacherous wandering. Finally, Aeneis arrives in Italy and founds the glorious city of Rome."

"Enough of ancient mythology," thinks the boy.

But the navigator goes on. "And then there's Dante's *Divine Comedy*, written in Italian in the 13th century CE where we first meet Pilgrim in *Inferno* — which is hell. But led by the lady Beatrice — which means 'beloved' — he finds that the way out of his imprisonment is through the spiritual and civil renewal of the whole of humanity. This leads him to *Purgatorio* — purgatory — where he must spend a long time struggling toward the light so that his spirit can be purified in order to be worthy to ascend into heaven. By the end of this struggle, Pilgrim advances to *Paradiso* — heaven — that is an earthly state of natural perfection.

"Now, no matter what the language or the period or the culture," explains the navigator, "the story is always the same. The hero finds himself in some kind of situation from which he must escape. It involves leaving his familiar world behind and embarking on a long and perilous journey. He must undertake the adventure alone — but he is not without aid. For once he commits to the mission, the gods assist him along the way. Then after enduring many difficult trials, he eventually reaches his goal.

"The interesting thing about this is that the hero is a very ordinary person who discovers along the way that he can do extraordinary things. Maybe the purpose is to tell us we were born for greater things than we are doing. And maybe that's why the interest in astrology has always run parallel to astronomy. The idea that perhaps our legend is written in the stars. And if we only knew how to read those stars, we would know the path we are to follow."

The boy knew his path. And he didn't find it by looking at the stars. So now he's a bit confused about the whole legend thing. "Is that the only way people can find their path?" he asks.

"Some people seem to know their personal legend," the navigator replies. "They have great dreams about what they want to do with their time on the planet. And then there are others who seem to have no dream at all; they more or less go along with things, letting others decide what they think and do. They hide their hopes, even from themselves."

"So what do all these old stories have to do with it?" the boy wants to know.

"Mythology reminds us that we are all on a hero's journey," comes the reply. "And it tells us that when we know our personal legend and follow it, the whole universe conspires to help us."

"Well, my legend," states the boy, "is to find the lost gold and take it home."

"I know," replies the navigator, "and the universe is conspiring to help you."

"How?" the boy challenges.

"Ah, that," the navigator proclaims, "I will tell you *manana.*"

THE JOURNAL

 Latitude   26° N
Longitude   41° W

DAY 5.   AT SEA

We are in the middle of the Atlantic Ocean now and the waters are absolutely calm. I can detect no wave patterns whatsoever. Indeed, the sea is as reflective as a mirror. If it were not for the enormous horsepower of our vessel, we would be completely becalmed. It makes me appreciate even more those early explorers who not only ventured into unknown territory but who did so wholly dependent on the winds.

How did Christopher Columbus manage to do it? What did he know of the winds, sailing as he did in unknown territory? Well, it turns out there was a closely held bit of information he discovered — or otherwise came to know about — that played an important role in his plans: in short, the trade winds! A brisk wind from the east, known as an "easterly", propelled his three ships, *Santa María*, *La Niña*, and *La Pinta* for five weeks from the Canary Islands.

That would serve his purpose sailing to the west, of course, but to return to Spain eastward against this prevailing wind would require several months of an arduous sailing technique, called beating, which uses a series of close-hauled legs to beat a course upwind.

A basic rule of sailing is that it is not possible to sail directly into the wind, simply because the angle of attack of the wind on the sail would be zero. I used to sail and took a number of basic navigational courses. I learned that, generally speaking, a modern boat could sail 45 degrees off the wind. When a boat is sailing this close to the wind, it is close-hauled or "beating to weather".

Because a boat cannot sail directly into the wind one can only get to an upwind destination by sailing close-hauled with the wind coming from one side, then tacking (turning the boat through the eye of the wind) and sailing with the wind coming from the other side. By this zigzagging method into the wind it is possible to reach any destination directly upwind. But at a price! If a boat can tack through an angle of 90 degrees upwind to an upwind distance of one mile, it would need to cover a distance of over 1.4 miles. An old adage describes beating as sailing for twice the distance at half the speed and three times the discomfort!

In the case of Columbus, beating his way back to Spain with three small ships would run the risk of exhausting his supply of food & drinkable water. So Columbus returned home by following prevailing winds northeastward from the southern zone of the North Atlantic to the middle latitudes of the North Atlantic, where prevailing winds are eastward (westerly) to the coastlines of Western Europe, and where the winds curve southward toward the Iberian Peninsula. As it turns out, Columbus was wrong about degrees of longitude to be traversed, and he was also wrong about distance per degree, but he was right about the most critical fact: how to use the North Atlantic's great circular wind pattern — clockwise in direction — to make his way home.

Imagine ....

THE JOURNAL

Latitude   28° N
Longitude   34° W

DAY 6.   AT SEA

We have left the Americas behind us now and
are cruising toward the great continent of
Africa. Interesting, when you think about it. We
praise the advances and achievements of Europe
— the great ideas of the Enlightenment and the
artistic genius of the Renaissance. But it was the
continent of Africa that gave rise to the human
family. Hominids there were going through an
evolutionary process at least 4 million, if not 5.5
million years ago. Like Australopithecus, the first
undoubted hominid, who lived between 1 and 4

or 5 million years ago. Fossils have been found in eastern Africa, in South Africa and as far away as Ethiopia's Afar depression. This early creature may have been primitive by hominid standards but he was a hominid nevertheless, physically if not culturally as well.

I wonder if the passengers on this good ship will realize our debt to Africa when they witness the great riches of Europe.

THE JOURNEY

Part III
AFRICAN GENESIS
Tracking the Human Odyssey

Imagine if you will, the beautiful *Legend of the Seas* in the middle of the vast Atlantic Ocean. Behind her, the great landmasses of the Americas recede. Ahead lay the vast continents of Europe and Africa. Imagine that in a few short days the ship will pass between those two great continents through a narrow channel of water and sail into the Mediterranean Sea.

It is night and the boy waits for the navigator to finish his watch. He cannot help but feel a twinge of excitement. Last night, as he gazed at distant stars and heard the legends of the great heroes, he began to sense that perhaps he too was on an extraordinary journey. The navigator had said that when people know their personal legend and follow it, the universe conspires to help them. And he is now beginning to believe that this man who directs the course of the ship is also directing the course of his life. The boy brims with anticipation as he sees the navigator approach, with the same crown and anchor pendant resting on his chest.

"In the great ports of the Mediterranean," the navigator begins, "the crowning achievements of Europe lay waiting. And you will see gold as you have never seen it before. But before you can make it your own, you must understand the path by which it travels. And the path begins not in the crown of Europe but in the continent that anchors it from below. Africa offers an important clue to finding gold — because gold follows the human odyssey and not the other way around.

"We don't know exactly how or when the human odyssey began," he continues, "but we do know that some of the earliest known human-like creatures were found in Africa and their bones date back at least 3 million years. The creature was called *Australopithecus* and there were two different species of them. One was *Australopithecus Robustus*. They had enormous molar teeth so they probably ate a vegetarian diet. The other, *Australopithecus Africanus*, was smaller and probably ate meat as well. At about the same time, another kind of 'ape-man' appeared. Anthropologists call him *'homo habilis'* which means 'handy man' because he used primitive stone tools. The tools were rough choppers and they were not fashioned in any way.

"Now we must fast forward all the way to five hundred thousand years ago before we find a more evolved creature. He gets the name *'homo erectus'* because he stands upright. *Homo erectus* has a bigger brain than *homo habilis* and is a somewhat more clever creature. He has mastered the use of tools and he cooks his meat with fire. Not only that, the tools he uses are shaped; they now have a cutting edge.

"But then the record gets blurred. *Homo erectus* seems to disappear and somewhere about 40,000 years ago, a new hominid takes his place. This one is more clever still and has an even bigger brain so he gets a new name. They call him *'homo sapiens'*, which means 'wise man'. And that is the creature which we also are."

At this very moment, the boy is not sure how the universe is conspiring to help him, but by now he has learned to stay silent and listen.

"Now," continues the navigator, " if we were to plot all this hominid history in a one-year calendar, *homo sapiens* would not even make an appearance until December 31st at 8 o'clock in the evening. You see, it is a very long path to get from standing upright to using tools to making tools to making fire."

The boy thinks the story is finished now.

"But that's only the beginning," the navigator states. "Let's now take just the creature *homo sapiens* and plot his 40,000-year history into a period of one year. 40,000 years ago is January 1st and, by this date, we can include the use of stone tools and fire. We can't tell from the fossil remains whether or not they had language but certainly some system of communication must have been in place by this time.

"Nothing much else happened in January — or in February or in March. By about the middle of April, we have evidence of carving. Nothing much else happened in May or in June or July. By August there is cave painting. That is a symbolic activity so it means they probably had language by that time because language is also a symbolic system.

"September comes; they domesticate the dog and by the beginning of October, we see the emergence of the first towns. This means they also have a capacity for agriculture and the storage of food surplus. And by the end of October, they have domesticated the horse.

"Things really get moving in November: metal work, the invention of the wheel, irrigation, the beginnings of ocean travel, the civilizations of Mesopotamia and Egypt, phonetic spelling and astronomy.

"And then comes December. So much happened in December that we have to divide the month into weeks and days. At the beginning of the month, we have iron working. By the end of the first week, there is the civilization of Greece, the ancient Olympic games, and your Mayan civilization. Two days later, we get the Buddha, the water wheel and Euclidian geometry. Two more days and we have Archimedean physics, a library at Alexandria and the civilization of Rome.

"The very next day, they invent the compass, along with the windmill and mathematics with a zero and a decimal system. Mohammed arrives the following day, along with paper, gunpowder, and the chromatic musical scale.

"By the last week in the month, we have Gutenberg movable type, the mind of Leonardo da Vinci, the art of Michelangelo, European global exploration, the plays of Shakespeare, the Brandenburg Concertos and the steam engine. The Industrial Revolution takes place on the 29th of December, along with the symphonies of Mozart and Beethoven, the American Constitution, and Realist and

Impressionist painting. By the 30th of the month, they add vaccinations, electricity, germ theory, photography, trans-ocean cable, telephone, radio . . . and the abolition of slavery.

"So much happens on the last day of the last month of the year that we have to divide it into hours. So December 31st at 2 a.m., they invent motion pictures and by 4 a.m., automobiles and aircraft. At 6 a.m., they reached the North Pole and the South Pole, develop IQ testing and discover vitamins. At 7 a.m. they build the Panama Canal. Two hours later, they discover penicillin, television and neutrons, and at 10 o'clock, they publish an anthropological study of sex in Polynesia. By 11 a.m., they add radar, the Rector scale and imprinting. By 12 noon, they discover the greenhouse effect, jet aircraft and DDT, and they are making blood transfusions, nuclear chain reactions, rockets and scuba diving equipment.

"Now it's 1 o'clock in the afternoon. They invent electronic computers, blood dialysis, LSD, the Green Revolution, the jet stream, fluoride and the microwave oven. By 2 p.m., they build a Polaroid camera, break the sound barrier, invent transistors and radiocarbon dating. 3 o'clock comes and with it, amniocentesis, the polio vaccine, the deciphering of the DNA helical structure, and the birth control pill. Oh, and in track and field, they break the barrier of the 4-minute mile.

"4 o'clock. They make a hydrogen bomb, a satellite, a pacemaker, a microchip and artificial intelligence. 5 o'clock. Now there are lasers and quasars, Valium and coronary heart bypass surgery.

6 p.m. Dinnertime. There's mega-vitamin therapy, catscan imaging of the brain, a ban on DDT, open-heart surgery, the geodesic dome, supply side economic theory, and the discovery of endorphins. And man rides to the moon on a spaceship he builds himself — but he comes right back again.

"7 o'clock ushers in a supersonic airplane, balloon angioplasty, a ban on chlorofluorocarbons and a test tube baby. It's 8 o'clock now. We see the eradication of smallpox, the first space shuttle, the discovery of the AIDS virus, genetically engineered insulin, the mechanical heart, and genetic finger printing. 9 p.m. We get the genetic sequencing of AIDS, Prozac, an abortion pill and Stephen Hawking's treatise on time and space. By 10 o'clock they add DNA mapping, the Hubble space telescope and in vitro fertilization. 11 p.m. They discover microbes on Mars, clone a sheep, build a computer program that can defeat a world chess champion, watch images on television as NASA roams the surface of Mars, and they create another new drug which is sort of the opposite of a birth control pill called Viagra. And now we're approaching 12 midnight and they are racing against the clock to meet the challenge of a two-digit simple coding error on millions of computers around the world.

"Now, tell me," he says to the boy, "what was it that accounted for all the advances in this human creature? Was it a yellow metal? "

The boy is silent. Gold, he realizes, was not mentioned even once.

"No," continues the navigator, "it was human imagination. Think of it. In this century alone, we have split the atom, probed the human psyche, altered genes and cloned a sheep. We have invented plastic, radar and the silicon chip; built airplanes, rockets, satellites, televisions and computers. We have overthrown our inherited ideas about language, learning, logic, mathematics, economics, even space and time. And behind each of these great ideas, great discoveries and great inventions is, in most cases, a single extraordinary human mind."

The boy is stymied. "But how can using my imagination help me to bring home the gold?" he begs.

"The same way it helped your Cristobal Colon. He followed the path of the human odyssey."

The boy is still puzzled.

The navigator explains. "Europeans used to believe the earth was flat. It kept them from doing and having a lot of things. Like sailing across the ocean and finding your gold. They were afraid they would fall off the edge of the earth. But people used their imaginations to figure things out. Like the Greek, Aristotle. He observed that the altitude of the stars changes according to the position of the person observing them. *Polaris* appears higher in the sky from Greece than it does from Egypt, and the brilliant star *Canopus* rises in Alexandria but is invisible from Athens. So he figured out that the earth must be round.

"Now Aristotle was not the first to have this idea. It was actually one of his countrymen called Anaximander. But this insight was not accepted, even in the freethinking Greek culture. It took another of their countrymen, a man named Pythagoras, to reinforce Anaximander's views before people would take it seriously. And that eventually led to Aristotle's experiments in astronomy, which provided the necessary proof.

"So, you see, when people use their imagination and challenge old beliefs, it creates whole new possibilities. Anaximander, Pythagoras and Aristotle played a part in Cristobal Colon's setting sail across the Atlantic in search of China and the East Indies. And that in turn led to the discovery of another whole new world of possibilities. It is true that he returned to Spain with metallic gold. But the real gold was the history of ideas that allowed him to make the extraordinary journey in the first place."

"Then why," asks the boy, "do people still put so much value on having gold?"

"Because," replies the navigator, "just as humans are the most evolved and therefore the most precious species in the animal kingdom, gold is the most evolved and therefore the most precious metal in the mineral kingdom. Where this principle is recognized, gold becomes a symbol for human evolution. And where it is not understood, it becomes a basis for human conflict.

"You see, alchemists have spent many a lifetime trying to turn base metal into gold. And they have never succeeded because alchemy is really just a code word. It stands for turning human beings into gold, turning our base qualities of ignorance and fear into wisdom and love. That is the most precious stuff there is."

The boy was not expecting this kind of answer. Perhaps he was now beginning to understand how every journey begins with beginner's luck and ends with the hero being sorely tested. Like all those heroes of ancient times, maybe he would emerge victorious. But right now he feels like this search for gold is pushing him up against a brick wall!

THE JOURNAL

Latitude	*28°* N
Longitude	*28⁸* W

DAY 7.   AT SEA

After these next two days at sea we will reach some island groups again, but this time they will be islands off the great continent of Africa.

The first will be the Spanish Canary Islands, located 180 miles from the African coast. Since antiquity, the Canary Islands have been a land of legends, and their existence can be traced back to Greek authors such as Homer and Plato. These seven islands used to be imaginary, known then as the Fortunate Islands. They remained mythological and mysterious until sometime after the Middle Ages.

It is believed that the first inhabitants in the Canaries arrived in the first or second century BCE. They had white skin, blue eyes and blonde hair, and were related to North Africa's Cro-Magnon man. They were cave dwellers, and like the ancient Egyptians, embalmed their dead, presumably for ceremonial passage into the next world.

In the early 14th century, a Genoese sailor by the name of Lanzarotto Marcello became the first European visitor. But the European conquest began in 1402, led by Jean de Bethencourt, under the service of Henry III, King of Castile. By the end of the 15th century, the Spanish had conquered all seven islands — but not without resistance from the Portuguese who also fought for ownership in the mid 1400's.

With the Canaries being the world's most westerly-charted point, the islands became the last stopping point for the explorations of Christopher Columbus before he ventured into the unknown. For the next several centuries, the Canaries served as a bridge between the Old World and the New.

THE JOURNAL

 Latitude   28° N

Longitude   21° W

DAY 8.   AT SEA

The day after we reach the Canary Islands, we will be making port in Funchal, the capital of the Portuguese island of Madeira, situated some 350 miles from North Africa.

Madeira was discovered by the Portuguese explorer Joao Goncalves Zarco in 1419. The Portuguese settled on the island and established trade links with Italy, Flanders and England. In 1560, the Spanish invaded Portugal and occupied Madeira. Portuguese sovereignty was not regained until 1640 — almost a century later. Strong ties were formed with England in 1662 when Charles II married Catherine of Braganca from Portugal's royal house. Many

British wine merchants came to settle in Madeira, resulting in wine production in the region. I wonder if the passengers realize the troublesome history of these two neighbours.

The last of five consecutive days at sea. Some of the passengers are growing restless now. Five sea days in a row seems to weigh on them. The next two days will change all that. Tomorrow, they will step ashore on a Spanish island, the following day on one belonging to Portugal.

Spain and Portugal: two powerful nations that once held enormous economic and political sway in Europe, undermined in the end not by any deficiency in ways or means but simply because of what they were thinking!

Imagine ....

THE JOURNEY

Part IV
ALL THAT GLITTERS
The Golden Days of Spain

Imagine if you will, that the ship is a day's sailing from a group of volcanic islands off the coast of Africa. And that one day later it will make port in yet another archipelago of subtropical splendour not that different from the first.

"Two archipelagos," the navigator tells the boy at the end of his watch this night. "The first the Romans referred to as the Fortunate Isles because of their great riches."

"Like the gold in St. Thomas?" the boy asks.

"You will not find there the gold of the Virgin Islands."

"But gold nevertheless?"

"Oh, yes."

"And by what name are these islands known today?"

"Here's a clue." And the navigator sings, "Yellow bird, up high in banana tree …"

"Jamaica!" the boy shouts.

"No."

"In Jamaica, they have this kind of gold that you roll up and —"

"No, not that. Think of a gold colored bird."

"Ah, the Goose Islands."

"Goose Islands?" repeats the navigator. "How did you get that?"

"I hear that the goose lays a golden egg."

"No, it doesn't!"

The boy is really thick sometimes. And he just can't get gold off his brain.

"It's the Canary Islands," asserts the navigator. "A perfect climate. Warmed by African winds in winter, cooled by the trade winds in summer. And they have magnificent scenic beauty, even a snow-capped mountain.

"These islands," the navigator continues, "have belonged to Spain for more than 500 years. The people there are mostly Spanish and they speak Spanish although they don't feel that connected to mainland Spain. We will be docking at Santa Cruz on the island of Tenerife. The town was founded in 1494, the same time Cristobal Colon was sailing in your part of the world.

"The following day, we will dock at Funchal in the Madeira Islands. They're not very far from the first group, and they're not very different: pleasant climate, sugar cane, vineyards …. But in another way they are a world apart — because these islands are Portuguese. They were colonized by Portugal in 1420 and they belong to Portugal today.

"Now there's something very interesting about this. Two sets of islands off the coast of Africa, sharing similar characteristics, and quite close to each other — but split between Spain and Portugal. It's a pattern we see again and again. If you look at a map of Europe, you will see that Spain and Portugal have split the Iberian Peninsula. And if you look at a map of the New World, you can see how they split South America too; Spanish-speaking in the one part, Portuguese-speaking in another.

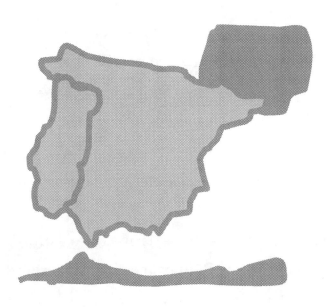

"Here you have the Iberian Peninsula, isolated by seas and mountains, subject to conquest from Europe on the north and from Africa on the south and with direct access to the Atlantic Ocean and all the wealth that lays beyond it. And it is here that Spain, with only Portugal as her neighbour, bears a history dating back half a million years.

"It starts with our early human species, *homo erectus*, migrating from Africa. Over time, he evolves to *homo sapiens*, paints some cave pictures, and learns to do agriculture and all that.

"Fast-forward now. First the Romans extend their empire into the peninsula from North Africa, then Germanic barbarians like the Visigoths move in. The Visigoths convert to Christianity and start some Christian kingdoms. Then the Muslims defeat the Visigoths and kill off most of the Christians, except for a few who manage to survive in the north. With the help of the French warriors under Charlemagne, the Christians eventually regain a bit of power. On and on … a Muslim kingdom here, a Christian one there, threats from the north and threats from the south ... a Spanish monarch takes over Portugal ... Portugal manages to free itself again ....

"Now we come to the 15th century and everything changes. Why? Because people dare to believe that the world is not flat. And when this happens, they are ready to look in the opposite direction for their wealth — and they head out into the sea. Prince Henry, the Navigator, from Portugal — who is the king's son — starts sending some ships into the Atlantic. Portugal colonizes Madeira along with the Azores. Before too long, the Portuguese captains venture farther from land and sail their ships down the west coast of Africa and round the Cape of Good Hope. What they want and what they are on their way to capturing is the spice trade of the East Indies.

"The Spanish — who are divided into a number of smaller kingdoms — quite naturally want to keep up with their neighbour. But there is no single kingdom strong enough to undertake this kind of exploration. The two most likely candidates are Aragon and Castile but they are busy fighting against each other and against Portugal.

"Now, by chance or good fortune, Isabella the 1st accedes to the throne of Castile and soon after, her husband Ferdinand the 1st comes to the throne of Aragon. Now the two most powerful kingdoms in Spain are joined — and presto! They outfit Cristobal Colon and off he goes, convinced he can beat the Portuguese to the East Indies by sailing in the opposite direction.

"But on the way, Cristobal runs into the Americas and arrives back not with spices but with gold. The Portuguese get wind of this, and now they're rushing off in both directions. But they are smart about it. First, they sign a treaty with Spain which gives them the right to explore the Atlantic route to the East Indies and to lay claim to lands to the east of a line running north and south through the upper part of South America.

"So the Portuguese reach Brazil and claim it for Portugal; the Spanish reach Peru and claim it for Spain. Everybody's happy. Fleets of Spanish ships and fleets of Portuguese ships crisscross the Atlantic, bringing home the gold. The wealth of the New World pours into the Iberian Peninsula, making these two neighbors the envy of each other and the rest of Europe.

"Now we come to the 1600's. Spain gets control of Portugal and they share the lustre for a while. But by the end of the century, their power and glory are gone. Spain loses her strength at home and drags Portugal into her wars. The Dutch take over Portuguese colonies in the East Indies and part of Brazil. Spain loses control of her colonies in America. Eventually Portugal resents Spanish wars and taxes, and feels that Spain is indifferent to her needs. This leads to rebellion and Portugal gets her independence from Spain.

"So, in spite of all the gold, Spain is eventually reduced to the status of a minor undeveloped nation while the rest of Europe is expanding because of the Industrial Revolution. And Portugal, for her part, ends up with what we might call an unfavourable balance of trade.

"Now, tell me, how, with all the gold in their possession, could they lose their wealth and power?"

The boy has no answer.

"Precisely because of it," explains the navigator. "In Spain, the influx of gold from America undermined the way people had created their wealth up to that point. So much gold poured in that it started to lose its value, and people came to place more importance on consumption than creativity. The kings, cajoled into complacency, passed on the duties of government to underlings who were unfit to manage. And the people lost the use of the very thing that had led them to create their wealth in the first place: their imaginations.

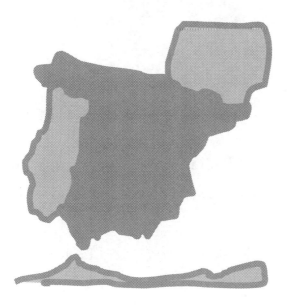

"Portugal fared no better. The discoveries enriched Lisbon and the court but depopulated the countryside as generations of energetic men ventured out, never to return. Almost none of the wealth was reinvested in Portugal, nor was it spread outside the small circles of the court.

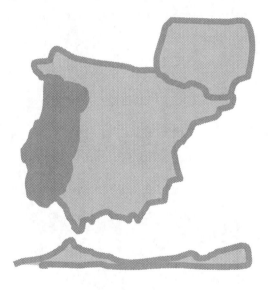

"Now, do you think your own people lost their wealth and power because they lost a yellow metal?" he asks the boy.

The boy is stymied. How else could they have lost it, he muses.

"Let's take a closer look at the great Mayan culture," the navigator continues. "By 5000 BCE they are settled along the Caribbean and Pacific coasts, forming egalitarian fishing communities. By 2000 BCE they have moved inland and adopted agriculture for their subsistence. They grow maize and beans as their main crops — same as today. They are also growing squash and tomatoes, peppers and fruits. A very good diet.

"By 1000 BCE, they are making pottery and carving in jade. Soon after, they start using astronomy, writing and the calendar. They even record their history in their own language.

"By 900 BCE they develop extensive trading routes to connect the farming villages and begin to develop intensive agriculture. These ideas and practices bring great prosperity and allow them to support a growing population. And it works for centuries. By 900 CE there may have been as many as 2 million people living in the Mayan area, and Tikel, the largest centre, may have had a population as large as 75 to 100 thousand people. To support their sizable population, the Maya expand their system of intensive agriculture. That's a remarkable achievement.

"But now, something else begins to happen: the towns and villages are no longer egalitarian, and we see the formation of a class society dominated by a small elite. All the wealth created by intensive agriculture, and profits from their long-distance trading, begins to be concentrated in the hands of a few people. In the lowlands, they clear the villages and replace them with large communities where the emphasis is on massive ceremonial activities. In the highlands, they erect huge stone temples that portray the Maya leaders as deities. And from this point on, the Maya rulers reign as divine gods. This gives them immense power and wealth.

"The rulers of independent city-states now start making war on one another, and strong families overtake weaker ones. Chronic warfare and social upheaval lead to things like famine and disease. And that's exactly what happens. These Maya cities and small empires all disappear by the 10th century. The Maya continue to live in both the highlands and on the coast, but, just like Portugal and Spain, their days of splendour are gone.

"All of this happened 500 years before Cristobal Colon set sail for the New World. When he eventually encountered some Maya in 1502, they were in their high dugout canoes trading cloth and some other goods off the coast of Honduras.

"Now, it is true that the Spanish who followed Colon plundered gold. But it was not the taking of a yellow metal that allowed them to overpower the civilizations they found in the Americas. I'm not saying that what they did was right. But the thing that allowed them to do it was the way they used that pyramid of ideas."

"Then why did they bother with gold?" the boy wants to know.

"Because of its lustre. Gold has always been a precious metal. Remember: first it was used as money, then it became a standard for money, then a symbol of money, and now a symbol of evolution. That is all well and good. But if the *lustre* of gold turns into a *lust* for gold, the result is deadly conflict.

"The Greeks," the navigator continues, "tell the story of King Midas, who has the luck to ask for whatever he wishes. He asks that everything he touches should turn to gold. The wish is granted. He plucks the twig of an oak tree; it is immediately gold. He picks up a stone; it turns to gold. An apple and it turns to gold. Ecstatic, he orders the preparation of a magnificent feast to celebrate the miracle. But when he sits down and touches his fingers to the food, it turns to solid gold. And when he tries to sip the wine, it turns into liquid gold. His little daughter, who he loves more than anything else in the world, comes to console him in his misery. But the moment he reaches out and embraces her, she turns into a lifeless golden statue.

"Gold is a powerful symbol of life energy," the navigator concludes. "But if we seek it only in the form of a lifeless metal, we, like King Midas, may bring upon ourselves and others, great misery and pain. Think about this as you continue your search."

"Okay," says the boy, "but how do I find this other kind of gold?"

"That," replies the navigator, "I will tell you —"

"I know, I know," interrupts the boy, "you will tell me *manana*."

THE JOURNAL

Latitude   28° N
Longitude   16° W

DAY 9.   TENERIFE

Early this morning we tied up to the dock in the port city of Santa Cruz de Tenerife. While the city itself has few tourist attractions, the coastal and interior landscape makes the island well worth a visit. In the centre of the island, for example, Mt. Teide, the highest mountain in all of Spain, reaches a height of 12, 198 feet. It is now part of Las Canadas National Park.

In Santa Cruz itself is the Plaza de Espana where one can find the tourist office and the local government headquarters, as well as the Museo Arqueologica with exhibits pertaining to the life and death rituals of the early Guanche society. But the real cultural and religious capital of the island is in La Laguna, the second largest town in Tenerife where one will find the cathedral of La Laguna and the Church of Our Lady of the Immaculate Conception dating from the early 16th century.

One of the better-preserved old towns on the island is La Orotava with its stately mansions, historic churches and cobblestone streets. The island also has some resort areas with beautiful beaches.

After a day exploring the Spanish ambience of Tenerife, I returned to the ship for the overnight voyage to the Portuguese island of Madeira.

THE JOURNAL

Latitude   32° N
Longitude   17° W

DAY 10.   FUNCHAL

Funchal, capital of the island of Madeira, situated in the warm waters of the Gulf Stream off the coast of North Africa. The island is lush and mountainous with a mild, sunny climate, which makes it suitable for the growth of a variety of exotic trees and plants.

The economy here is based on a number of exports: bananas, potatoes, onions, orchids — and wine. Madeira is famous for its wine, which has been exported since the 17th century. And tourism flourishes. There are two local craft specialties as well: wickerwork and embroidery.

There are a few things to see in the town itself. The Governor's Residence—a palace dating from the 16th century—overlooks the pier. It is the home of the Minister of the Republic so not open to the public. A Museum of Sacred Arts contains a collection of religious sculptures and paintings from many of the Island's churches. The Cathedral, built during the late 15th and early 16th centuries, has a remarkable carved wooden ceiling depicting discoveries made by the founders of the Island. There is also the Collegiate Church of St. John, built by the Jesuits and dating from the 17th century, with its elaborate façade and beautiful baroque style interior. And not to be missed — a visit to the Madeira Wine Lodge to sample the local produce. Then there is the local market and the fish market, the Museu das Cruzes, occupying the house where Joao Goncalves Zarco, the Island's founder, is thought to have lived. It contains furniture, porcelain and paintings as well as relics taken from ancient buildings, surrounded by gardens with varieties of orchids. In the Chapel & Convent of Santa Clara is the final resting place of Zarco. The Convent is now a school run by Franciscan nuns. There is also a Municipal Museum close by the Convent.

What I most enjoyed doing in this town was strolling along the narrow streets looking at the array of local craft, and I was amazed at the intricacy and abundance of embroidery. Now a relaxing evening aboard ship and preparation for another lecture tomorrow.

THE JOURNAL

Latitude   35° N
Longitude   9° W

DAY 11.   AT SEA

At sea once again, this time for only one day. Tomorrow we will reach the southern coast of Spain and arrive at Malaga, known to many as the capital of the Costa del Sol, the "Sun Coast".

Settlement in the region can be traced as far back as the 4th millennium BCE when prehistoric man inhabited caves throughout Andalusia. In 3000 BCE, Iberians crossed over to Spain from North Africa, giving the peninsula its name. About 1100-800 BCE, Phoenicians established permanent trading posts along the coast in competition with Greek merchants. The Greeks and the Phoenicians were the first civilized inhabitants, followed by the Romans who occupied Spain until the 5th century CE.

In 711 the Moors invaded Spain from nearby Africa, bringing with them their Muslim religion and influence. The battles took over 10 years and in the end Cordoba became the new capital of Islamic Spain.

Independence for the Spanish was gained in the latter part of the 9th century, and Andalusia underwent a period of growth and development, with the building of a vast fleet of ships and the defeat of various Mediterranean territories. Wealth was reflected in the building of churches and the production of great works of art. It was during this time that Spain reached dominance in Europe.

As the Moorish empire disintegrated into fiefdoms, Christians began the long struggle to oust Muslims from the peninsula. In 1212, the Moors were defeated, and retreated to the kingdom of Granada. Nearly 300 years later, in 1492, Granada fell and Spain was unified under the Catholic Monarchs, Ferdinand and Isabella. It was the very same year Christopher Columbus set sail for the New World.

Imagine, if you will....

THE JOURNEY

Part V

RENAISSANCE AND ENLIGHTENMENT

The Real Gold of Europe

Imagine if you will, the *Legend of the Seas* cruising toward the Strait of Gibraltar. Tomorrow it will pass through the narrow channel at the point where the Atlantic Ocean meets the Mediterranean Sea. The boy knows the ship will soon anchor in Barcelona and his journey will be over. He waits on the deck, anticipating the final meeting with his mentor.

"Gibraltar is a British territory," begins the navigator on this memorable night. "It stretches for 3 miles into the Mediterranean Sea at the southwestern tip of Spain. You will see a very prominent rock with steep cliffs and a low isthmus a mile long, connecting it to the mainland.

"Gibraltar on the European side," he continues, "and Mt. Abyla in Morocco on the African side, have long been known as the 'Pillars of Hercules'. According to mythology, the great hero created the Strait by splitting and pulling apart the two mountains to let waters from the Atlantic Ocean flow into the Mediterranean Sea.

"The Strait of Gibraltar is a very strategic location that has always been a prized military possession. It has been conquered by Phoenicians, Carthaginians, Romans, Vandals, Visigoths, Moors, Spanish and British. Today it's a British crown colony. There is a fortified city on the Moroccan side of the entrance too. It's called Ceuta and it belongs to Spain. It was founded by Phoenicians, and then captured by many of the same forces — Carthaginians, Romans, Vandals, Byzantines, Arabs and Portuguese.

"So much warfare! And when we get to Malaga on the southern coast of Spain, you will see more evidence of warfare: an 8th-century Arab fortress on top a hill and the Alcazaba, another fortress constructed in the 8th and 9th centuries. Malaga also has a history of successive invasions.

"A lot of this Mediterranean warfare took place in the Middle Ages, which was the period after the fall of the Roman Empire, around 400 and before the year 1400. This was a period of a thousand years in which nothing else of real significance happened. There were no inventions apart from the water wheel in the 800's and the windmill in the 1100's. No startling new ideas appeared; no new territories outside Europe were explored. Everything was as it had been for as long as the oldest European could remember.

"The only world they knew was Europe with the Holy Land at one edge and North Africa at the other. They thought this world was at the centre of the universe. The sun moved round this flat Earth every day. Heaven was above and hell was below. Kings ruled at the pleasure of God; everyone else did what they were told. All knowledge was already known — and nothing was ever going to change.

"But then everything did change. All of a sudden, great discoveries, great inventions and great works of art appear. Like the printing press — which made knowledge available to vast numbers of people beyond the clergy and ruling elites. In 1456 there were fewer than sixty copies of the Bible, which was the first book printed in Europe. By 1500, less than 50 years later, there were more than fifteen million Bibles in circulation.

"Along with the printing press came the pencil, and inexpensive paper — which made writing, note-taking, and therefore the recording of learning accessible to common people. Also the magnetic compass, the astrolabe and the large sailing ship — which resulted in the expansion of ocean travel, international trade, and exchange of information. And the mechanical clock — that stimulated commerce by allowing people to think of time as something that could be managed. In the Middle Ages people had no concept of time as we know it. The vast majority of them didn't know what year it was or even what century they lived in.

"Why? Why, after a thousand years of nothing special do all of these things suddenly begin to happen?"

"Why?" echoes the boy, confident the navigator has the answer.

"Because something else happened that made people really stop and think. It was the Bubonic Plague, a disease that swept across Europe. Almost half of the population died a quick and horrible death because of it.

"And not just peasants, serfs, and tradesmen but also priests, bishops, and nobles. People started to realize that being pious and giving loyalty to a church or a king would not give them protection. Priests and nobles died alongside peasants and tradesmen in equal number. This really shook their faith. The church and the king would never be able to hold power over them again. People needed answers from outside the established institutions. They would no longer accept without question the things they had been told.

"So they started to think for themselves. They developed curiosity and a quest for continuous learning. They started to test knowledge through experience and learn from their mistakes. They began to rely on their own senses to cultivate their experience. They became willing to live with uncertainty. They strove to create in their lives a balance between science and art, and between logic and imagination. They cultivated grace and beauty, fitness and poise. They came to recognize and appreciate the interconnectedness of all things. After a thousand years of no new ideas, there is an awakening to all these new principles.

"The new movement was known as the Renaissance which means 're-birth'. It ushered in the Modern Age after a thousand years of the Dark Ages in Europe. And it paved the way for great inventions in the 17th century — and the Enlightenment a century after that. The Enlightenment championed the rational human being who was a philosopher, a writer, an artist, and a critic of established institutions all in one. Because of the ideas of this period, people learned to think for themselves, and to change the things about their society that were corrupt and unfair. Of course, they created some new problems as they fixed some old ones, but that was all part of the evolutionary process.

"You see, the thing they were figuring out is that they should never underestimate their own capabilities. Human beings are gifted with virtually unlimited potential for learning and creativity. We possess not only one kind of intelligence, measurable by a single IQ test. We have at least seven intelligences. And if we use our brains properly, we can actually improve our intelligence as we age.

"Do you know that your brain is more flexible and multidimensional than the most powerful computer? It is capable of learning seven facts per second, every second for the rest of your life—and there would still be room to learn more. Not only that, your intelligence is not only in your brain; it's in every cell of your body.

"Think of the logical and mathematical intelligence that allowed Pythagoras and Aristotle to figure out that the earth is round. And that led to the development of calculus, and mathematics with a zero and a decimal point. To physics and the laws of motion and gravity, and to the scientific method itself. And the great advances in astronomy and computer science.

"Look at the verbal and linguistic intelligence that allowed Homer and Virgil and Dante to write great mythologies, that produced the plays of Shakespeare, that allows us now to record our stories and histories.

"What about the spatial and mechanical intelligence that allowed early hominids to make tools and do cave paintings, that helped the Egyptians and the Maya to build their great pyramids and temples, that produced the wondrous sculptures of Michelangelo, that led to the building of automobiles, aircraft and the geodesic dome.

"Think of the musical intelligence that went into creating the diatonic and chromatic scales, the brilliant works of Bach and Handel, of Mozart and Beethoven, of opera and song and musical theatre.

"Then there is the bodily and kinesthetic intelligence that created the great athletes of the ancient Games and our modern Olympians today, the poise and beauty of the Renaissance man and woman, gymnastics, the martial arts, ballet and modern dance.

"Look at the interpersonal intelligence that ushered in the period of Enlightenment. The humanistic ideals of men like Rousseau and Voltaire in France, of Jefferson in America. The intelligence that led to the abolition of slavery, and throughout history, the humanitarians and philanthropists who strive to make the world a better place.

"And then there is intrapersonal intelligence — true self-knowledge — exemplified in the stories of people like the Buddha, Moses, Jesus, Mohammed. And scores of human beings who pursue a conscious path so that wisdom and light may triumph over fear and darkness, and, in so doing, advance human evolution.

"So you see," concludes the navigator, "there are seven intelligences for you to use in your search for gold."

The boy is silent. The journey he thought would soon be ending he now realizes has only just begun.

THE JOURNAL

Latitude   37° N
Longitude   4° W

DAY 12.   MALAGA, SPAIN

We have arrived in Malaga, on the Costa del Sol, a popular destination for visitors from all over Europe. In the past, the Costa del Sol was known for its tiny fishing villages. These villages have now been replaced with large retirement and resort towns, and Malaga is now home to more than half a million residents.

    Beyond Malaga is the famous region of Andalusia, stretching across the south of Spain and including such famous sites as the Palace of Alhambra, the Moorish palace that the locals refer to as the eighth wonder of the world. Built *during the 12th century in the city of Granada, it served as a fortress until it became a fortress-palace for the Nasrid Dynasty. I toured the Alhambra on a visit to Granada some years ago and it is truly a treasure. It has two main parts: the Alcazaba (the fortress) and the Casa Real (Royal Palace). The many rooms throughout the palace include the "Hall of Streets" where a whisper can be heard from any part of the chamber. This fortress-palace has survived many wars, including the Napoleonic occupation in the 18th century when it was nearly destroyed.*

Of course, Malaga has an outstanding palace-fortress of its own, and that's where I spent the better part of the day. The Muslim Alcazaba dominates most of the city centre. Started in 1057, it was the official residence to the Arab Emirs of Malaga who ruled the Kingdom. Seen on a hilltop from anywhere throughout the city, the fortress offers excellent views of the downtown area. The Alcazaba includes an archaeological museum, which adds to the historical and cultural richness of the place. I stayed a long time at the Alcazaba, gazing at the magnificent view and enjoying the ambience.

I also paid a visit to the Picasso Museum, located in a lovely 16th century building devoted to the Malaga-born painter, and where his daughter-in-law donated a large part of the collection. I made a stop at the House of Picasso as well. It was one of his first houses, and it was here that the artist discovered his love of painting. His entire family lived in this house for the first 14 years of his life, until they moved to Barcelona.

Everything I saw today was worth the visit, but it is the Alcazaba that will dominate my memory. For the Alcazaba symbolizes both the strength and the downfall of... imagination.

THE JOURNAL

Latitude   38° N
Longitude   1° E

DAY 13.   AT SEA

It is our final day at sea. Tomorrow we will make port in Barcelona and this will mark the end of the journey.

Barcelona ... with its Plaza del Rey in the Gothic Quarter ... where Christopher Columbus was welcomed by Isabel and Ferdinand when he returned from the New World ....

Barcelona ... the end of the journey ... or is it the beginning ....

THE JOURNEY

Epilogue
THE WAY HOME

Imagine if you will, it is the evening before the end of the cruise. The boy knows it is his final meeting with the navigator. He listens carefully to the parting words of the man who he now truly realizes has not only been directing the course of the ship but also the course of his life.

"When the ship docks in Barcelona," suggests the navigator, "go to the Plaza del Rey in the Gothic Quarter. There you will find the place where Cristobal Colon was welcomed by Isabel and Ferdinand when he returned from the New World with your gold. Then, go to the harbour. There you will find the Santa Maria, a replica of the small ship Cristobal Colon used to make his journey.

"Now, ask yourself this question. Which is the real gold: the handful of metal he brought back with him, or the fact that, in spite of major errors in his navigational calculations that took him to an unknown place where he did not intend to go, he was able to find his way home again?

"You are the navigator of your own life," the navigator concludes. "Seek out your personal legend and make a plan to follow it."

"And when I have the plan?" the boy asks.

"Set your coordinates," comes the reply, "and fix your course to a star. Then, like all the other passengers on this good ship, find your way home again. You see, the journey is always to find your way home. Because home is both the origin and the destination."

"If that is the case," asks the boy, "then why make the journey at all?"

The navigator smiles and quietly replies, "To bring home the gold." And with that he removes his crown and anchor pendant and gives it to the boy.

THE JOURNAL

Latitude   41° N

Longitude   2° W

DAY 14.   BARCELONA

Our beautiful ship, home for the past two weeks, has brought us safely across the Atlantic and we arrive at our port of disembarkation on schedule in the early morning. When we are cleared to go ashore, I depart the ship and walk along the dock toward the city.

And there it is, right in front of me: the Monument a Colon. The tall column, reaching into the sky, dominates both the harbour and the skyline: One cannot miss it! The statue of Columbus himself, atop the tall column faces not inward to the land but outward to the sea.

The Monument a Colon marks the beginning — or is it the end — of Las Ramblas, a tree-lined pedestrian boulevard stretching all the way from the waterfront to Playa Catalunya. Off to the right of Las Ramblas is the Gothic Quarter, with medieval buildings dating from the 13th century. It was here that Columbus met the King and Queen of Spain when he ended his first journey. I wander the narrow streets, imagining the scene and pondering his state of mind. Did he realize what he had achieved? After all, he failed to do what he set out to do — and what those backing the venture expected him to do. Did he eagerly greet the King and Queen, expecting to receive praise for a crowning achievement? Or did he approach with trepidation, anticipating a royal rebuke for a monumental failure?

I wander back to the waterfront, and enter the Maritime Museum that occupies the Royal Medieval Dockyards. There are a number of marine exhibits here. Among them are those describing Columbus' four voyages. The record is one of crowning achievements.

Columbus could not have known that the world would remember him this way, that his crowning achievement would turn out to be not what he set out to do but what he discovered along the way. It reminds me that when we do not achieve what we set out to do, our crowning achievement might also be what we discover along the way. As in the case of Columbus — and the young cabin boy in my story — what we are destined to do in life may turn out to be far greater than we could imagine. I now realize that surrendering to that deeper purpose is what it really means to bring home the gold.

ACKNOWLEDGEMENTS

Anyone familiar with the outstanding work of anthropologist Joseph Campbell will immediately recognize my indebtedness to him. Indeed, it was because of his writings about the mythological hero's journey that I felt inspired to create this modern Mayan hero myth for the benefit of travellers who journey from the New World to the Old. I have since created a modern heroine myth based on Viking origins for travellers journeying from the Old World to the New.

Thank you also to my editor Ken Johnson for help and support along the way. He has been my right hand man on this and numerous creative projects. I also acknowledge the people at Trafford who have guided me through the publication process for this and previous books. Special thanks to Royal Caribbean for inviting me to lecture on their beautiful flagship, and to all the cruise passengers and readers of my work for their abiding interest in the power of myth.

ABOUT THE AUTHOR

Pamela J Peck is an author, lecturer, composer and playwright whose professional interest is education for a global perspective, and the application of social science knowledge to the practical concerns of everyday life. Canadian born, she holds the degrees of Bachelor of Arts in Psychology and Religion (Mount Allison University), Bachelor of Social Work, Master of Social Work and PhD in Anthropology (UBC). She was a Research Associate at the University of Delhi in India and a Post-doctoral Fellow at the University of the South Pacific in Fiji.

Pamela has traveled to more than 100 countries around the world, and has lived and studied in many of them. She uses her cultural experiences to infuse and inform her novels, short stories, screenplays and stage musicals. Drawing on the archetypal structure of classical mythology and Jungian psychology, her creative works embody timeless and universal principles. Her stories appeal to people of all ages as she takes us on magical and adventurous journeys to the far corners of the outer world, and into the inner recesses of the human mind.

Printed in the United States
By Bookmasters